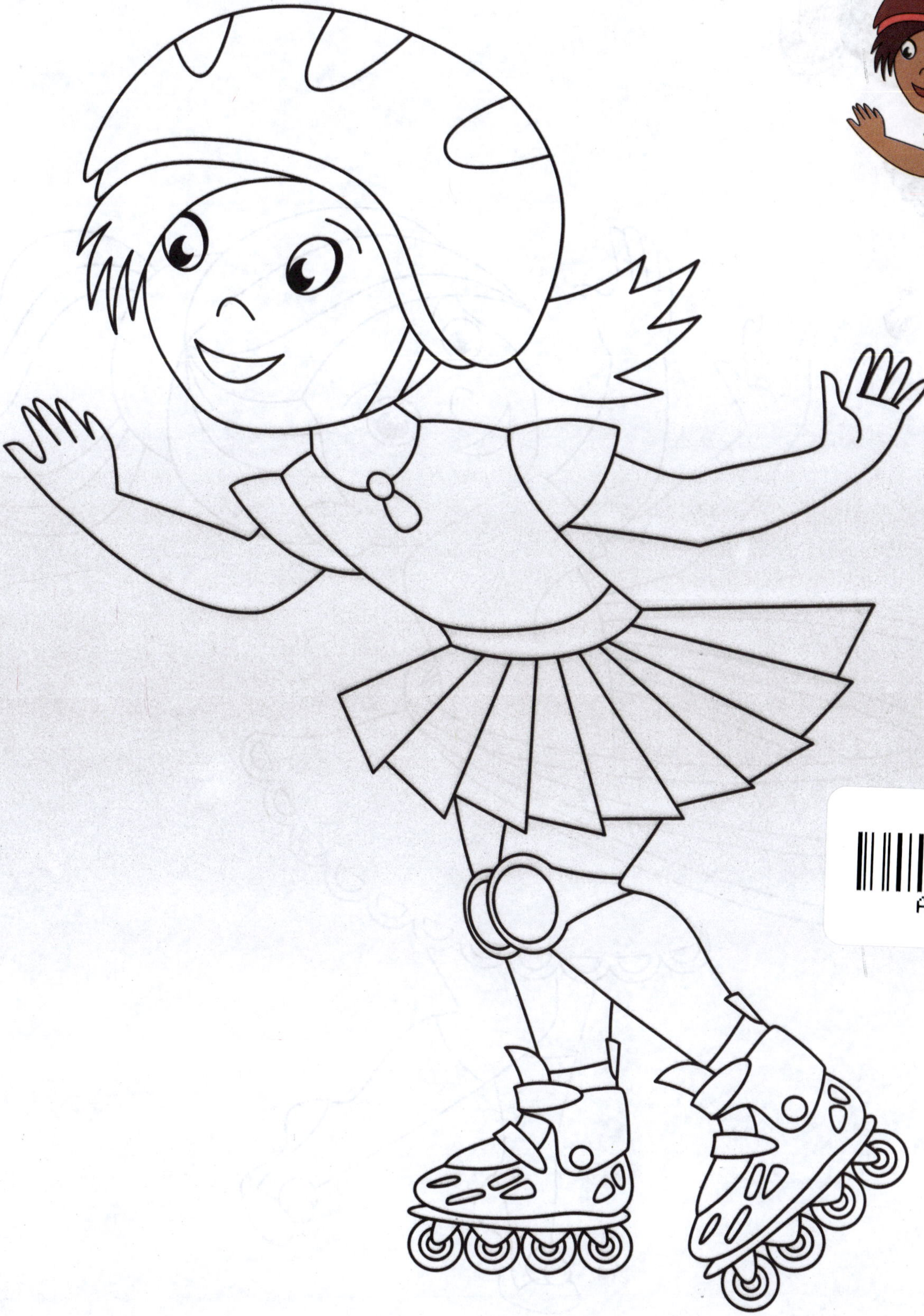

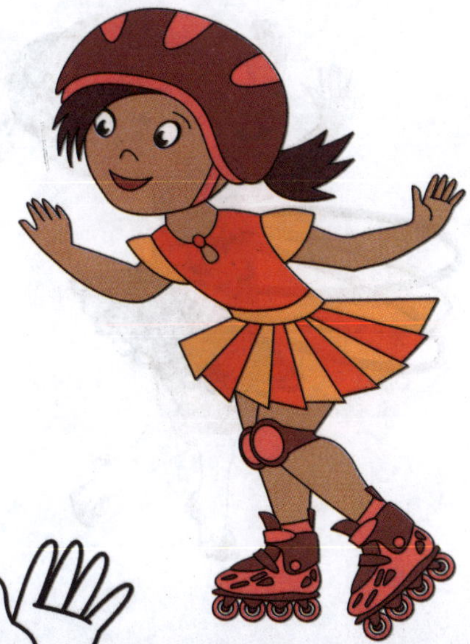

roller skating

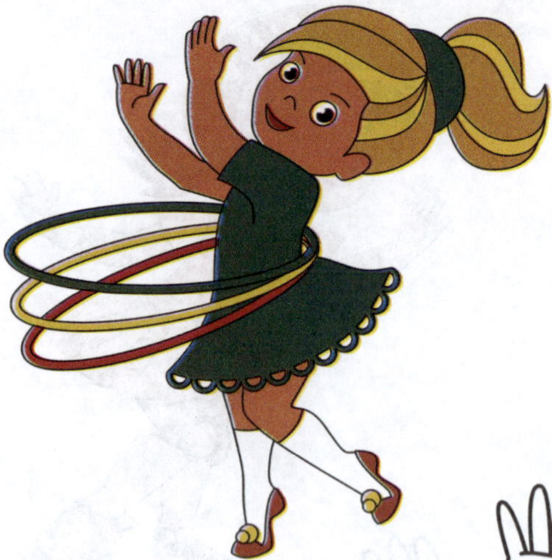

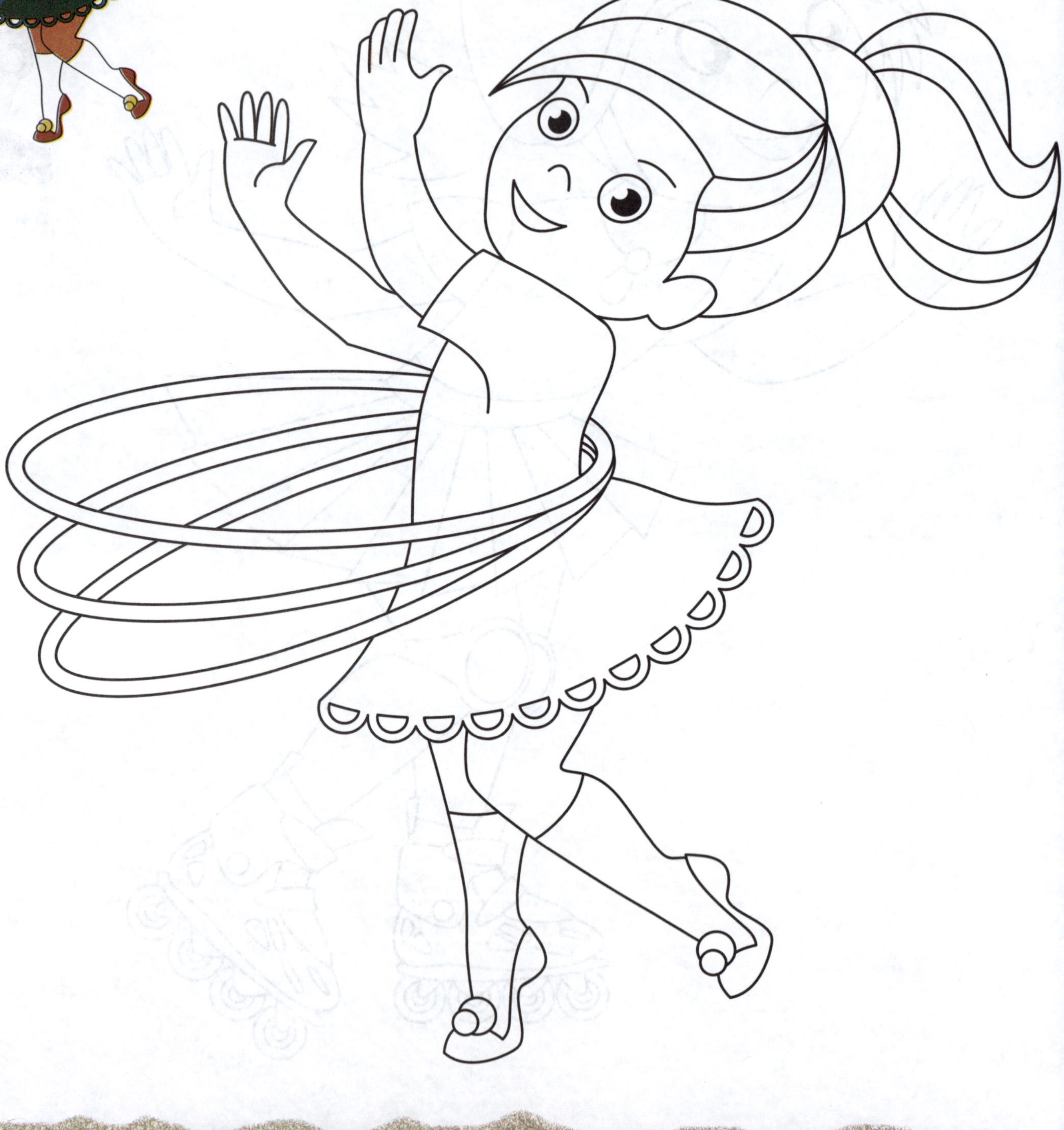

hula hoop

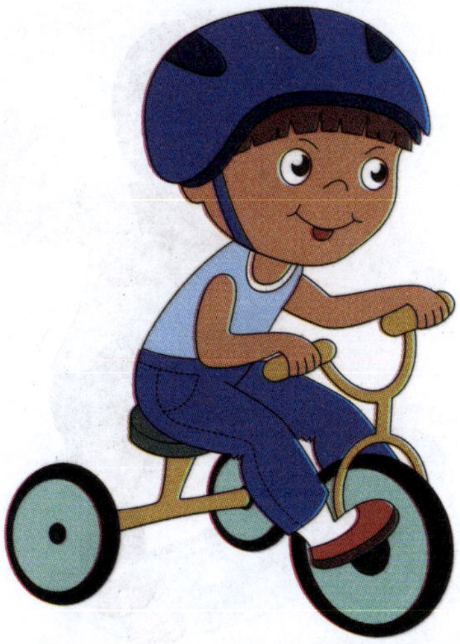

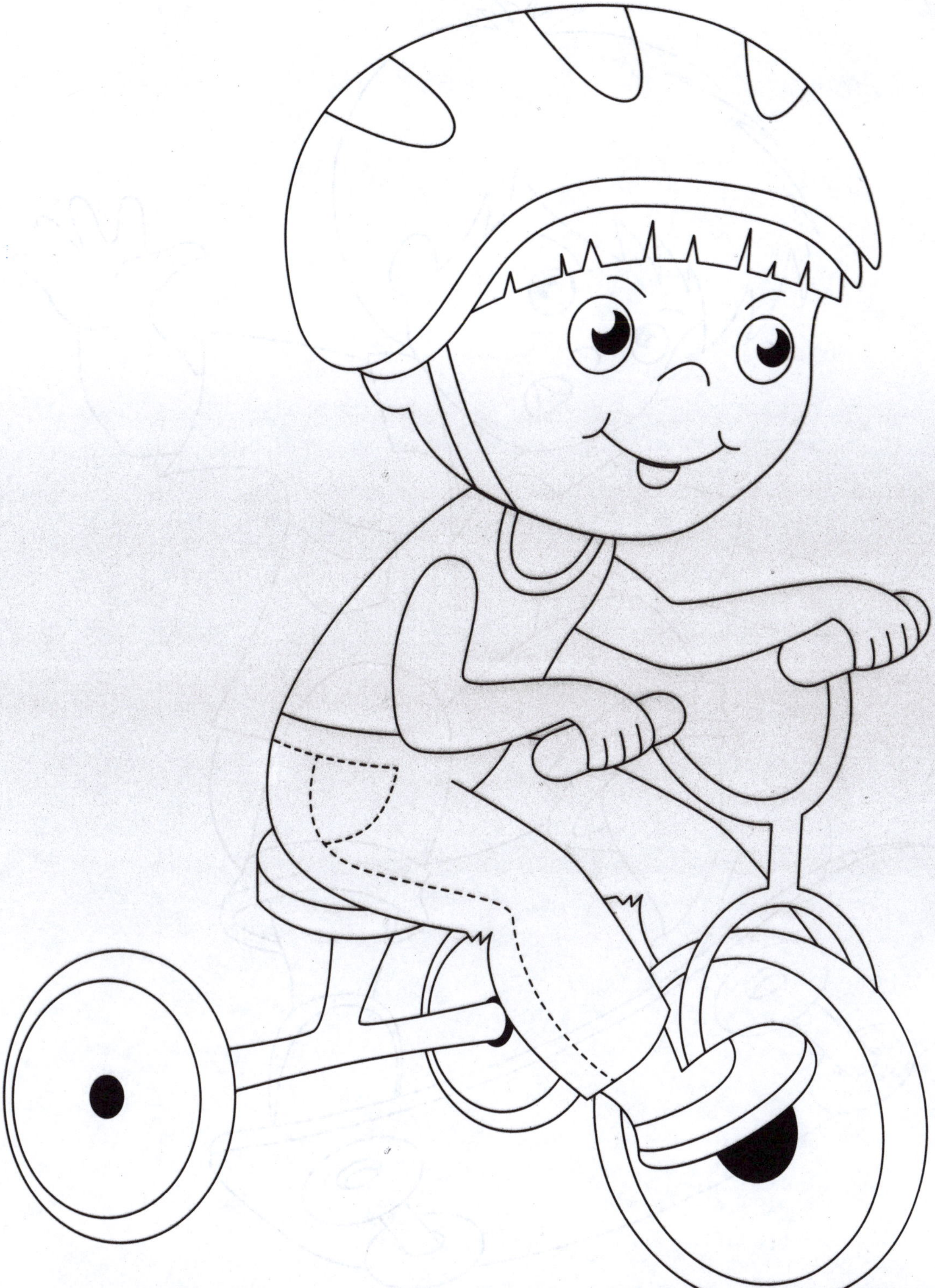

cycling

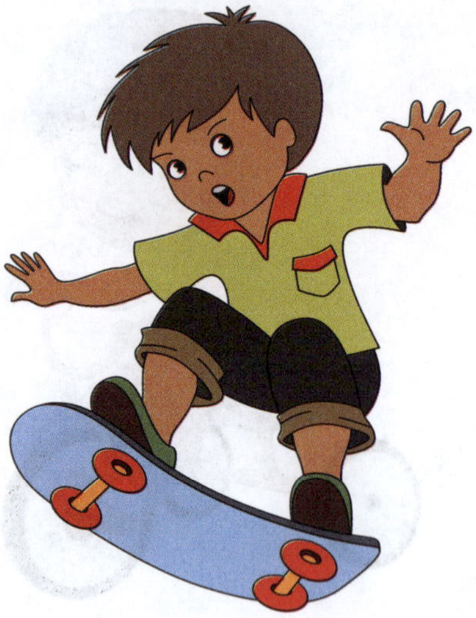

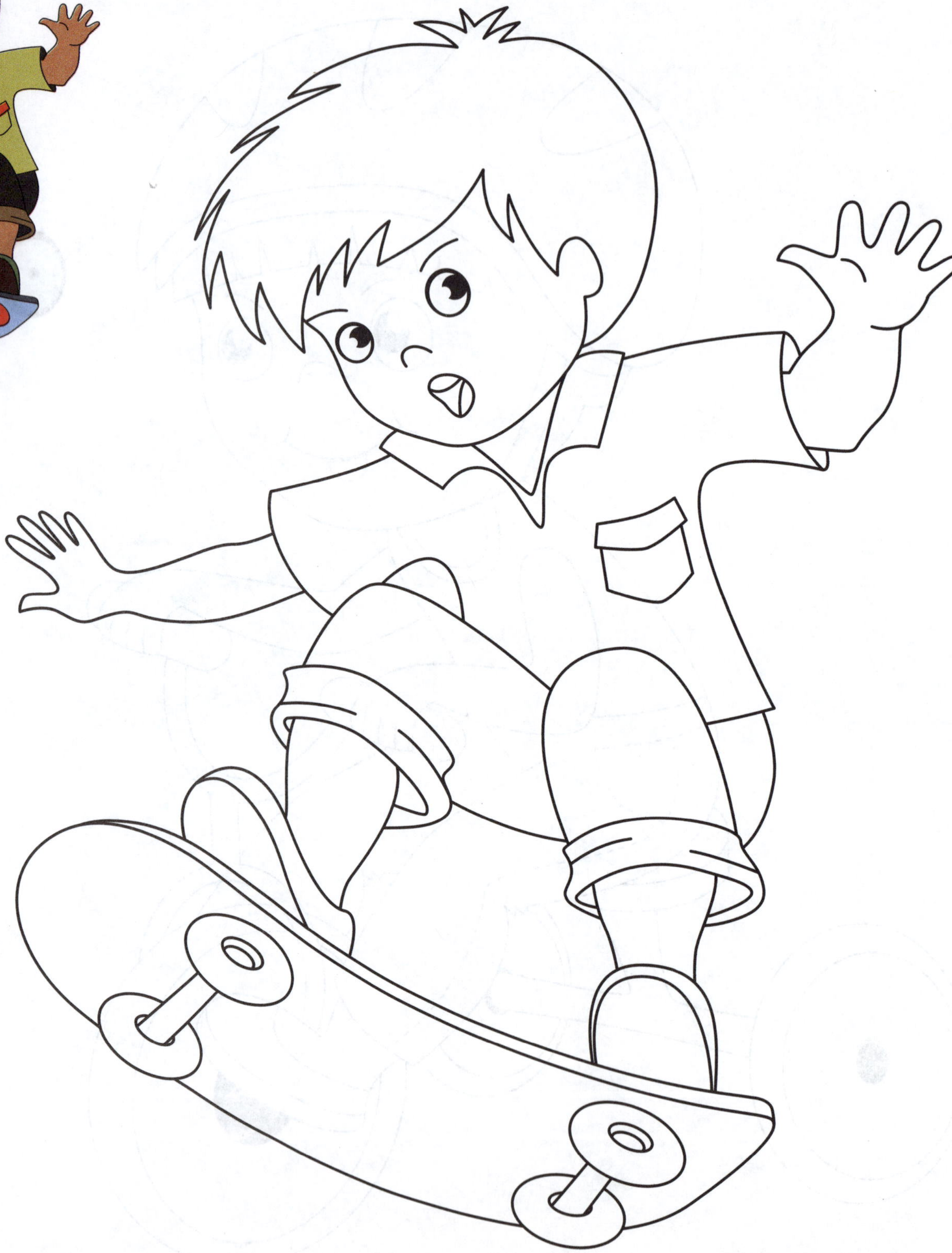

skateboarding

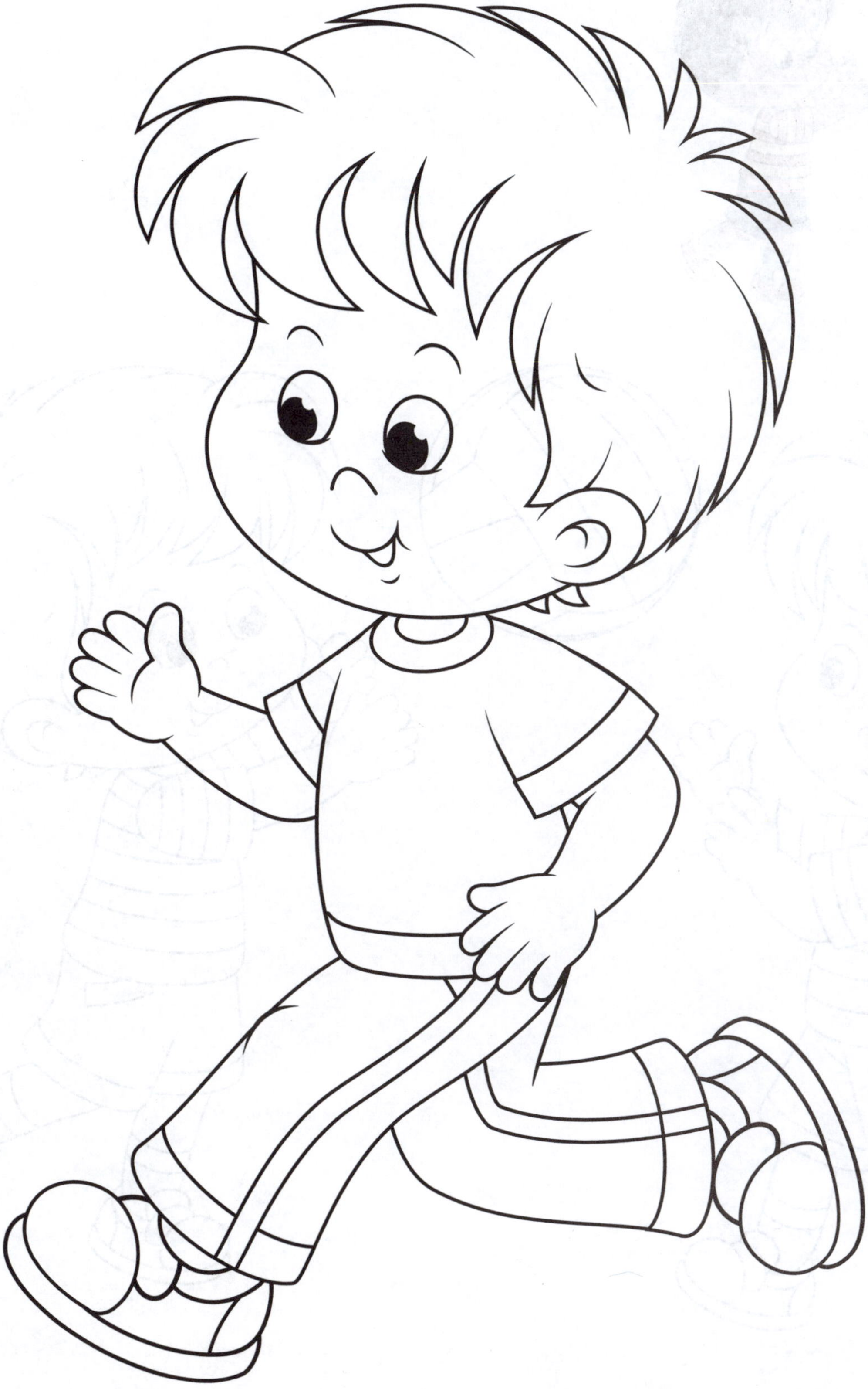

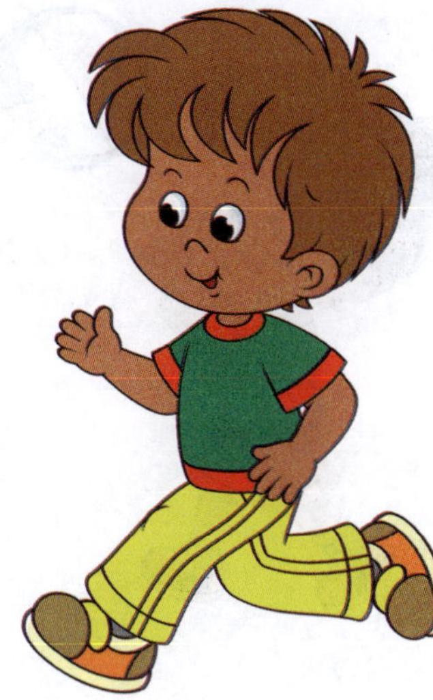

running

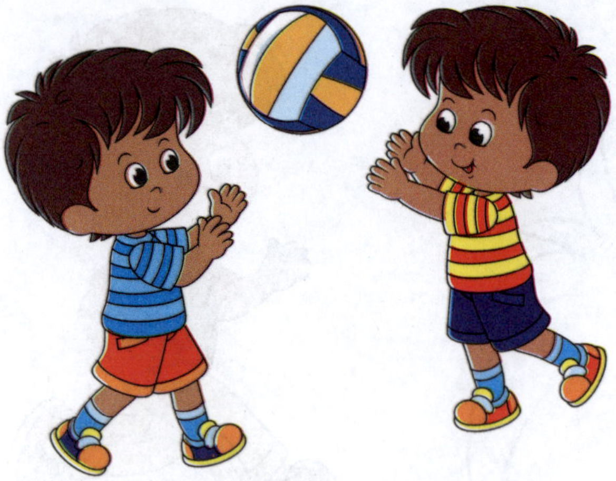

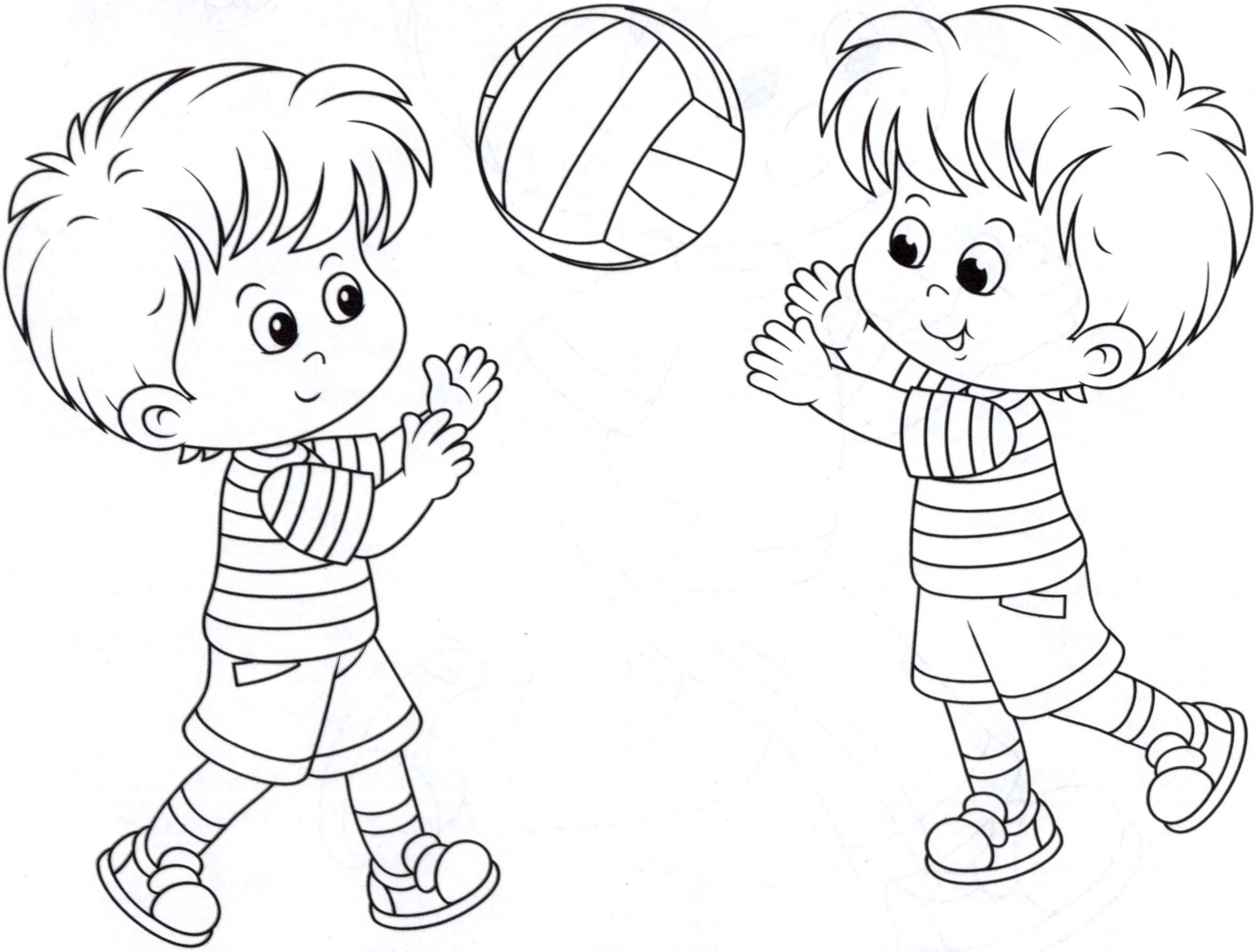

volleyball

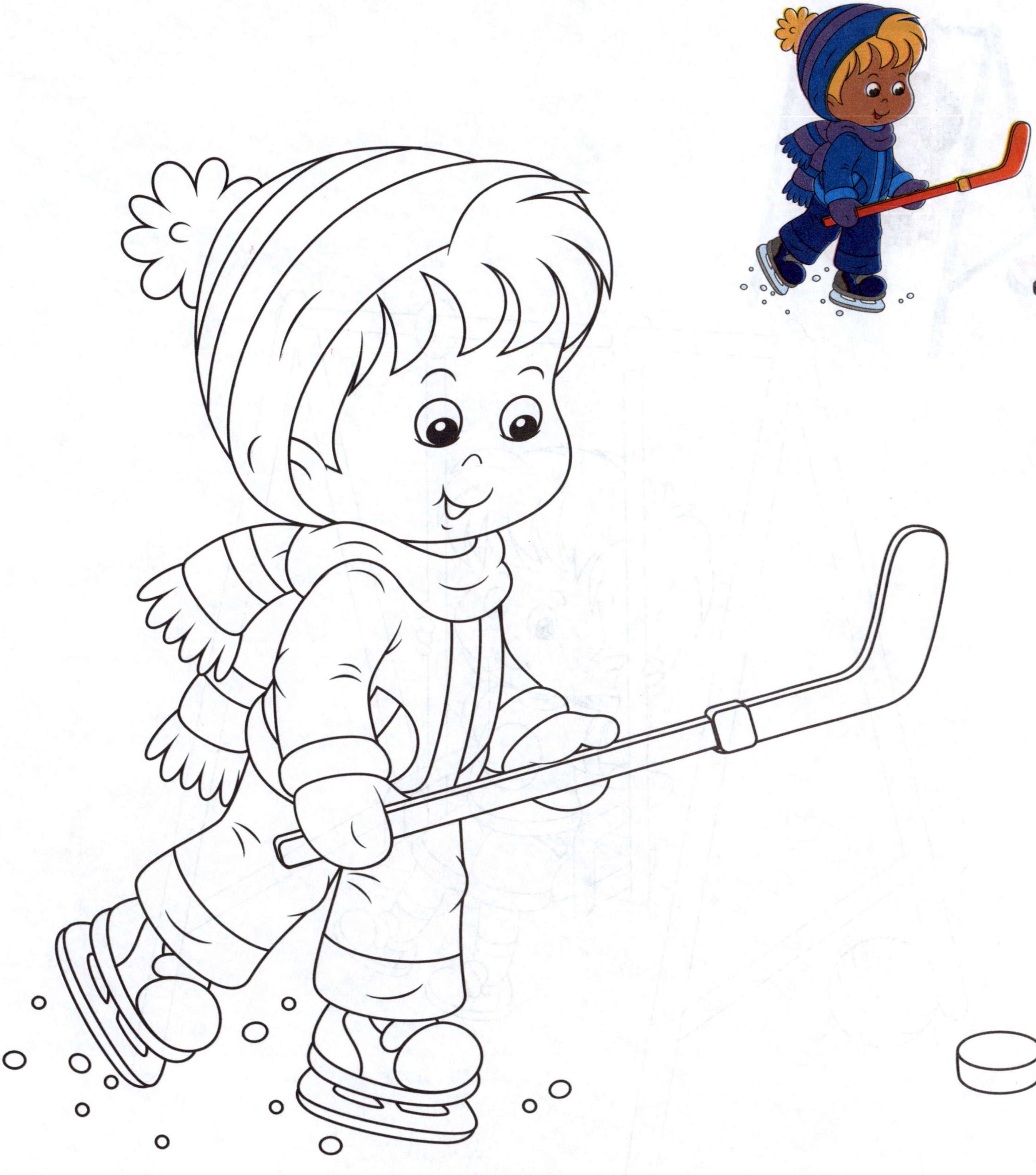

ice hockey

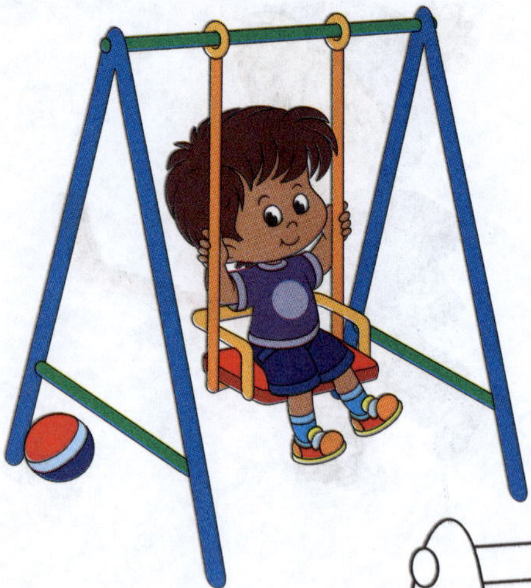

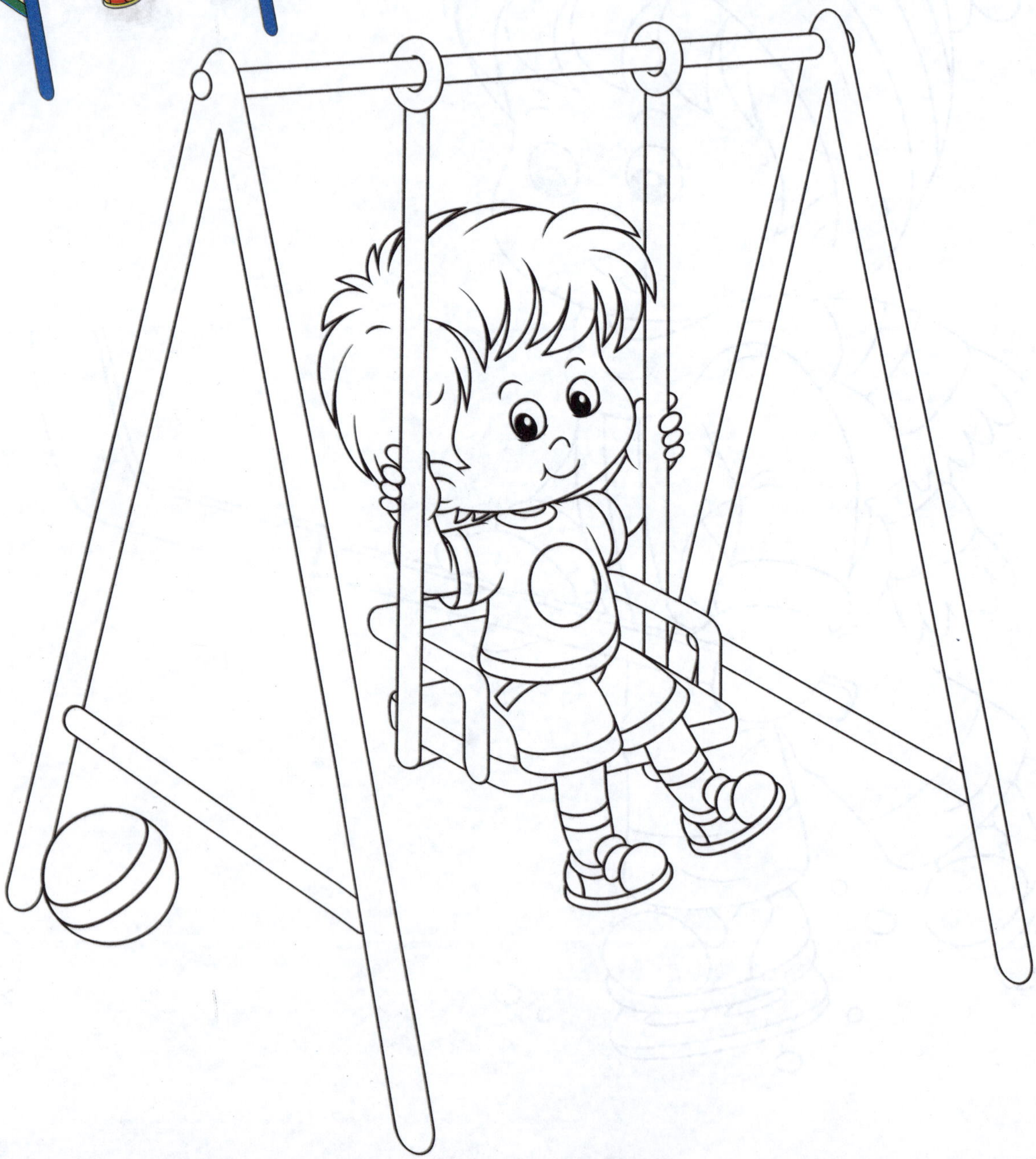

swing

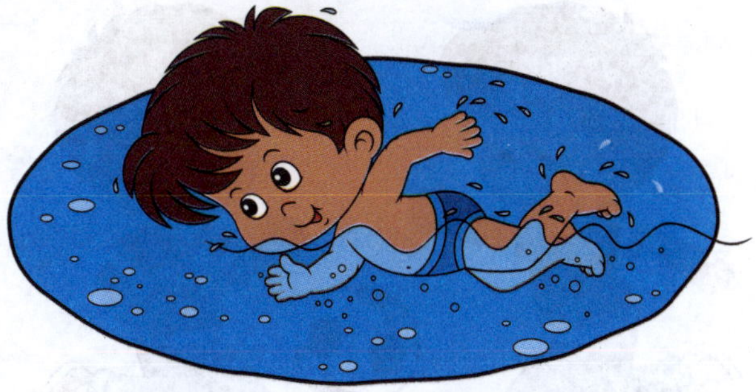

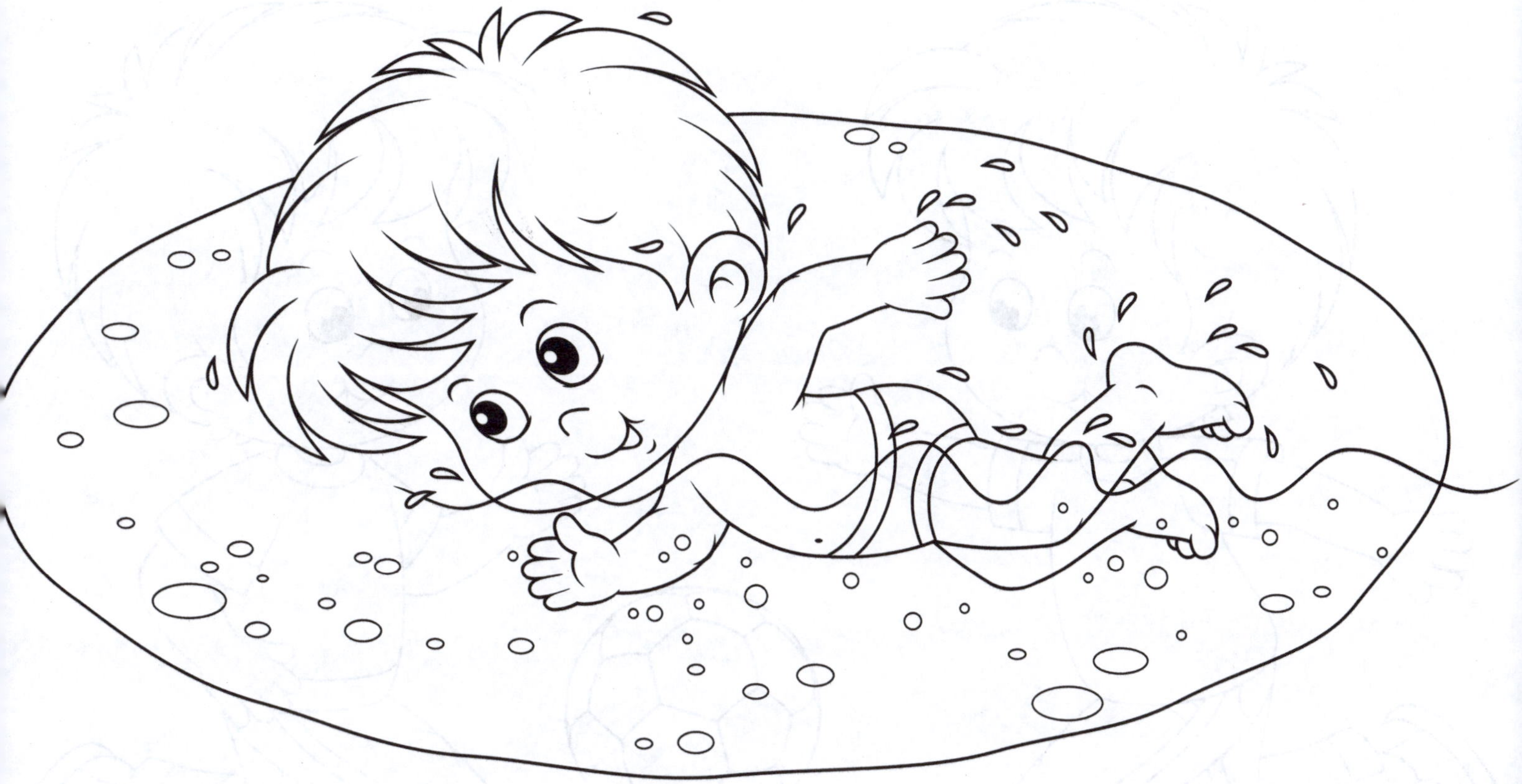

swimming

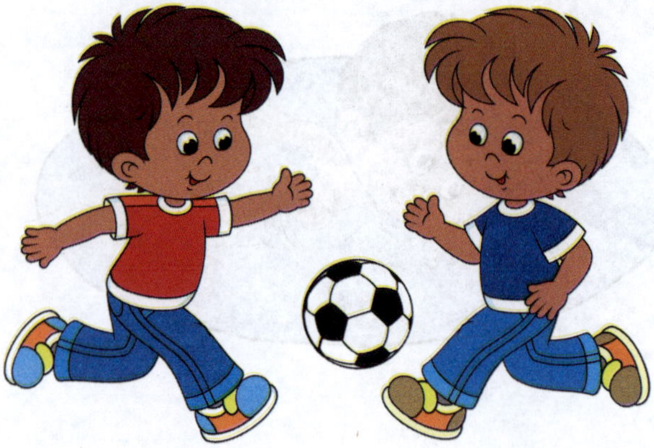

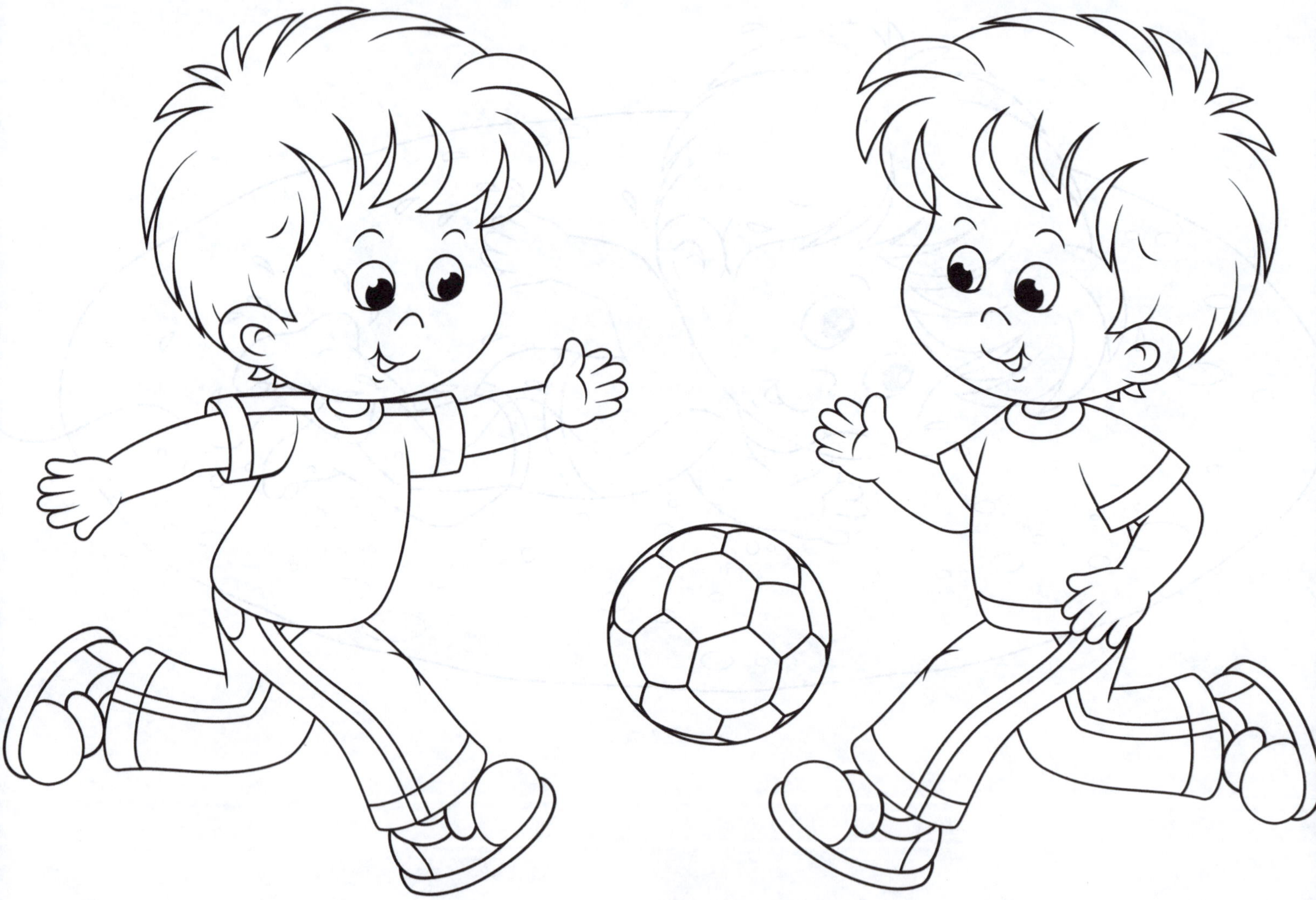

football

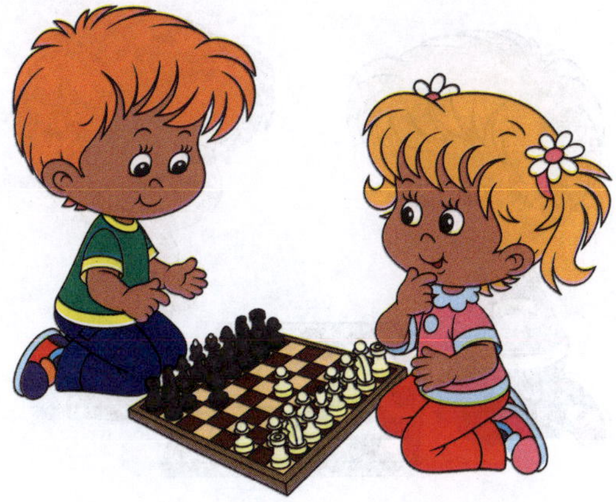

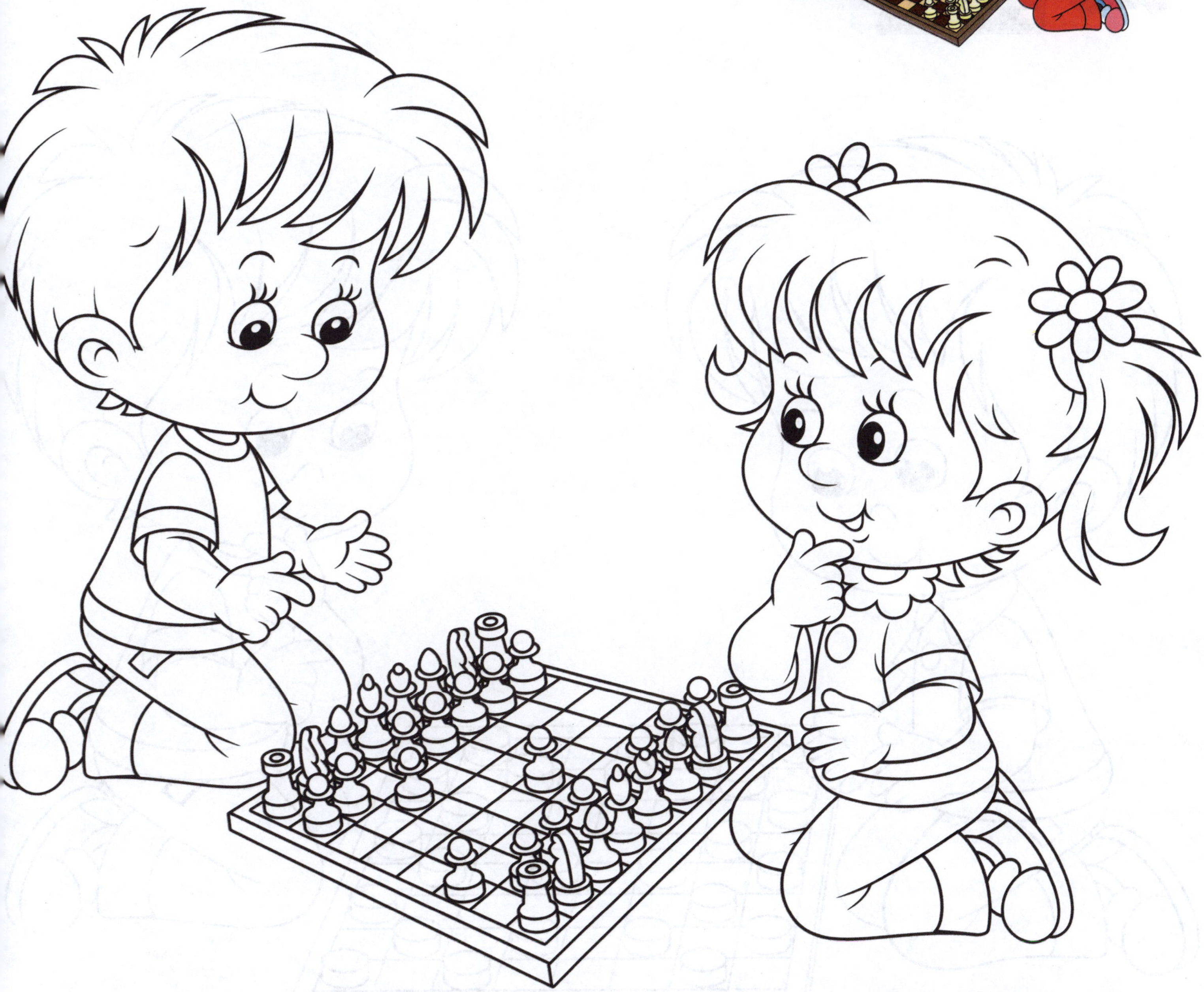

chess

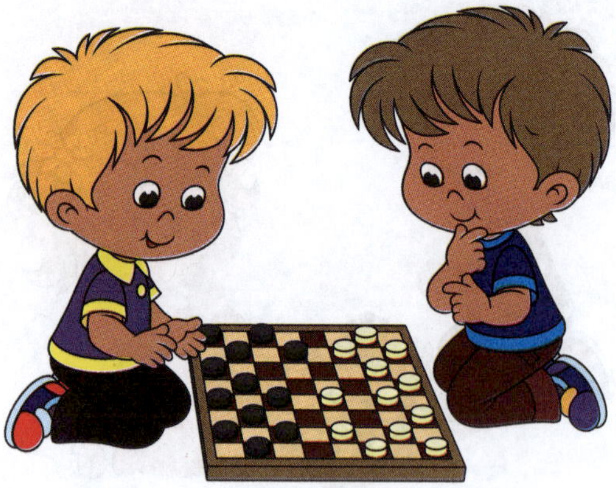

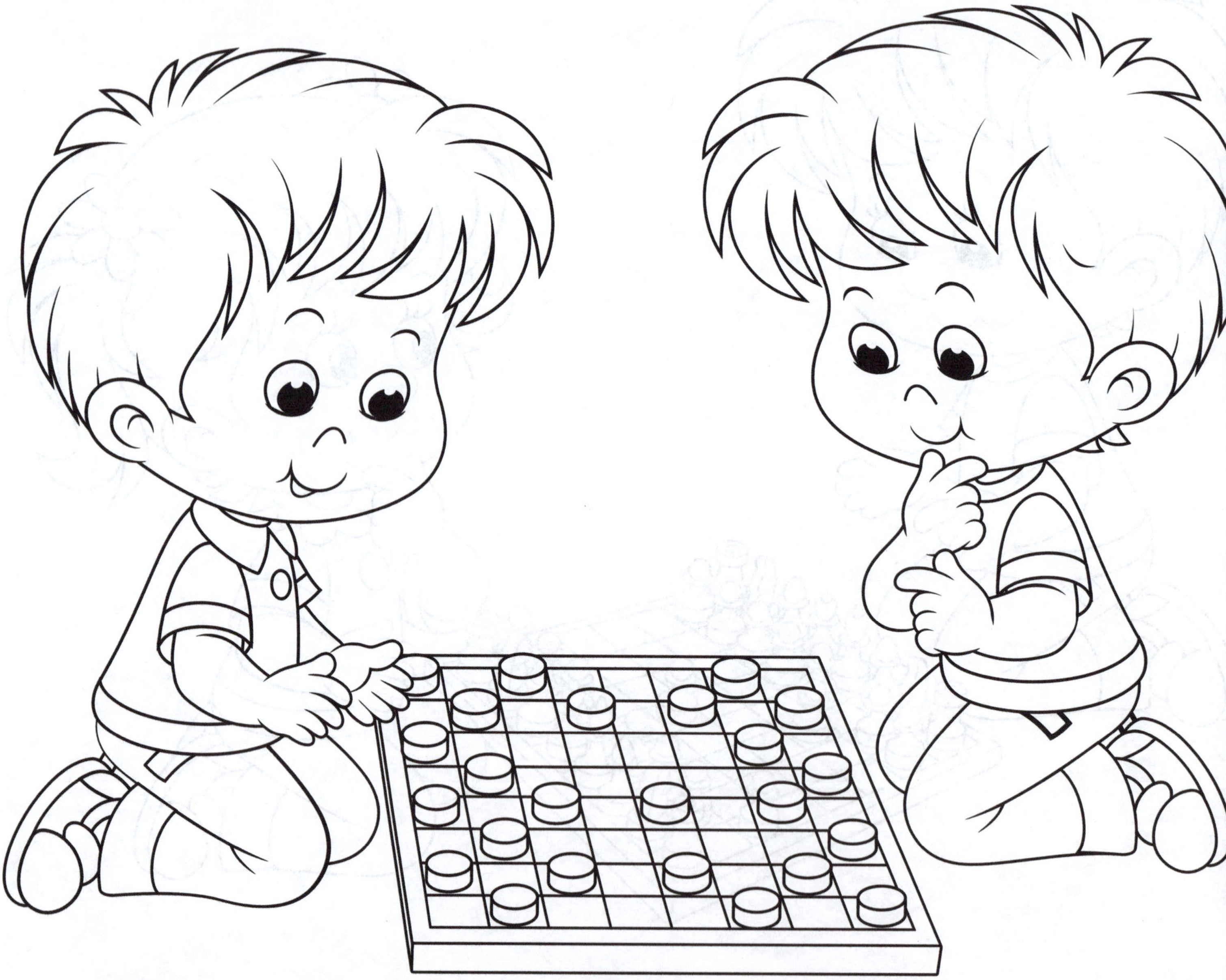

checkers

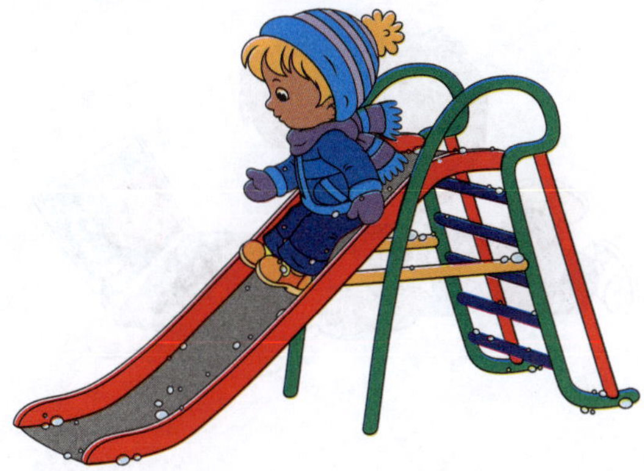

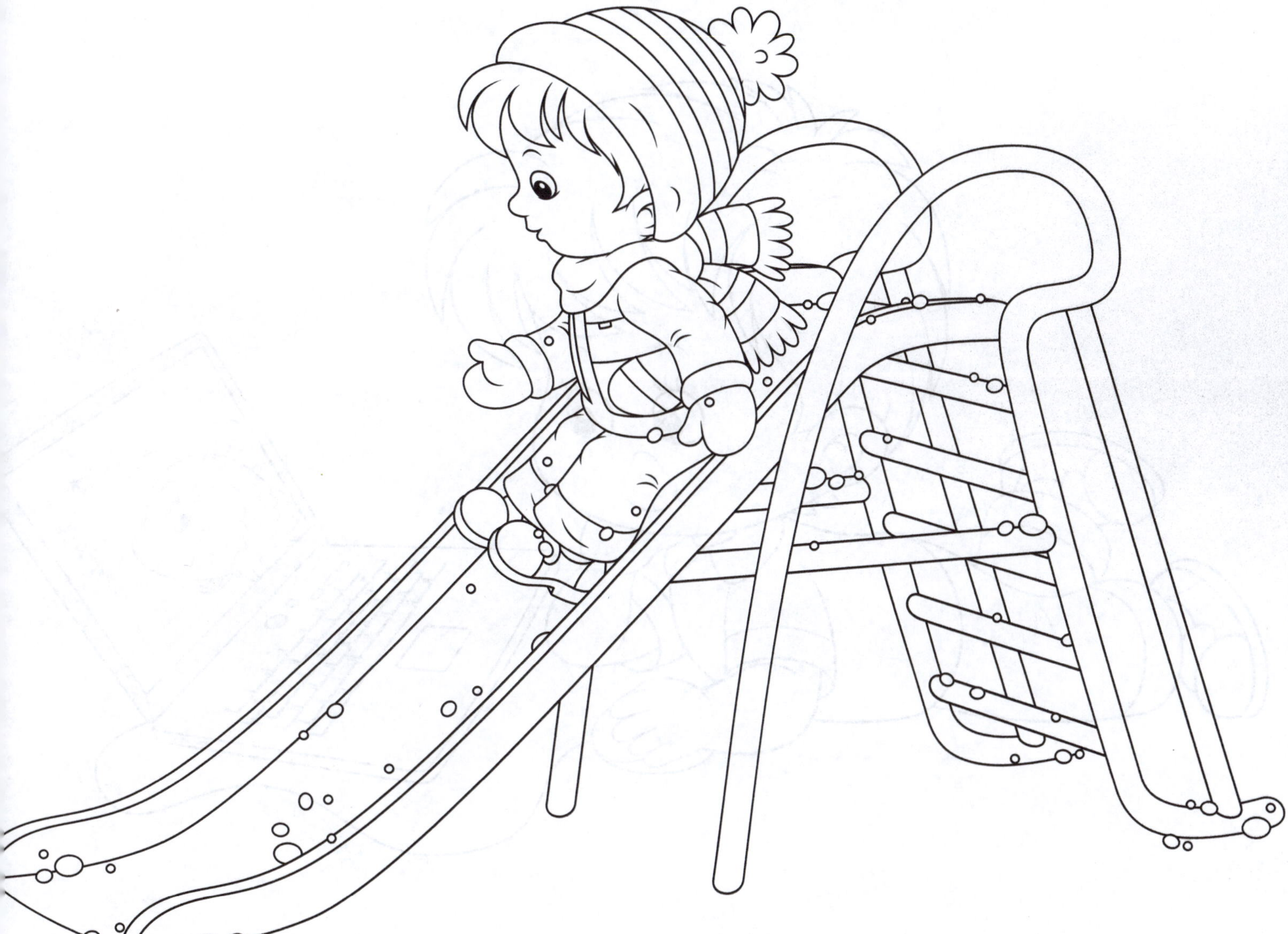

slide

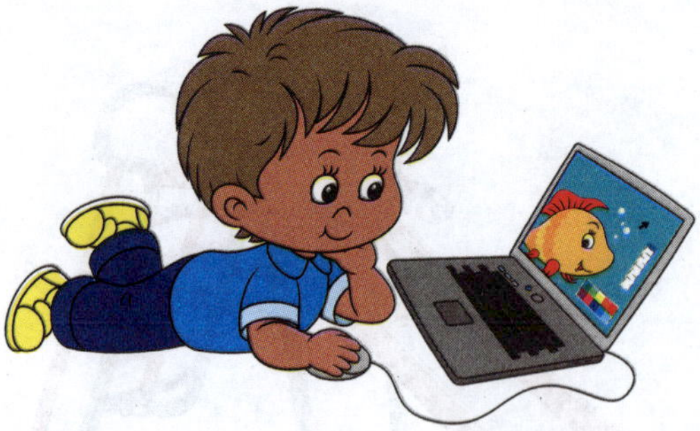

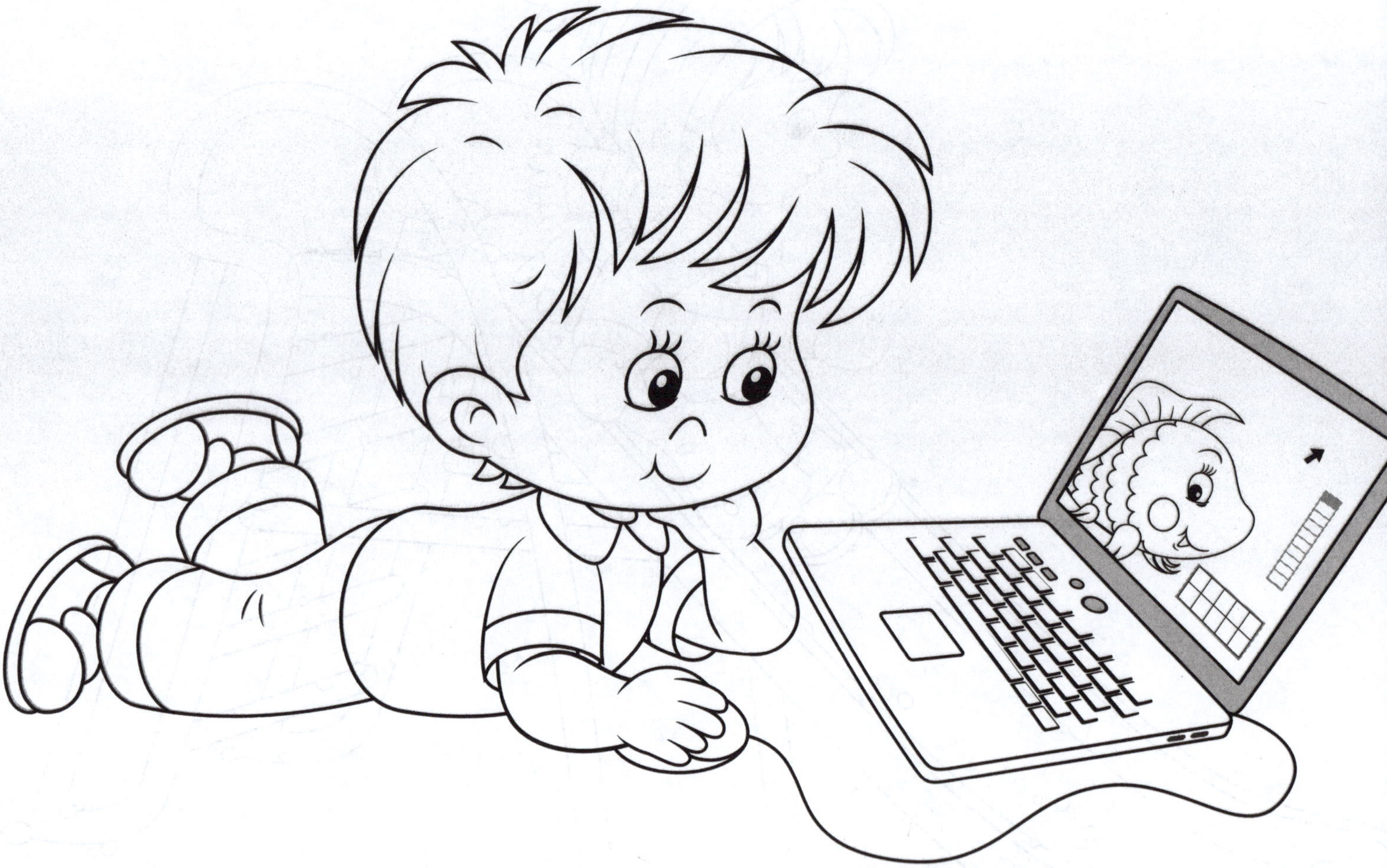

computer game

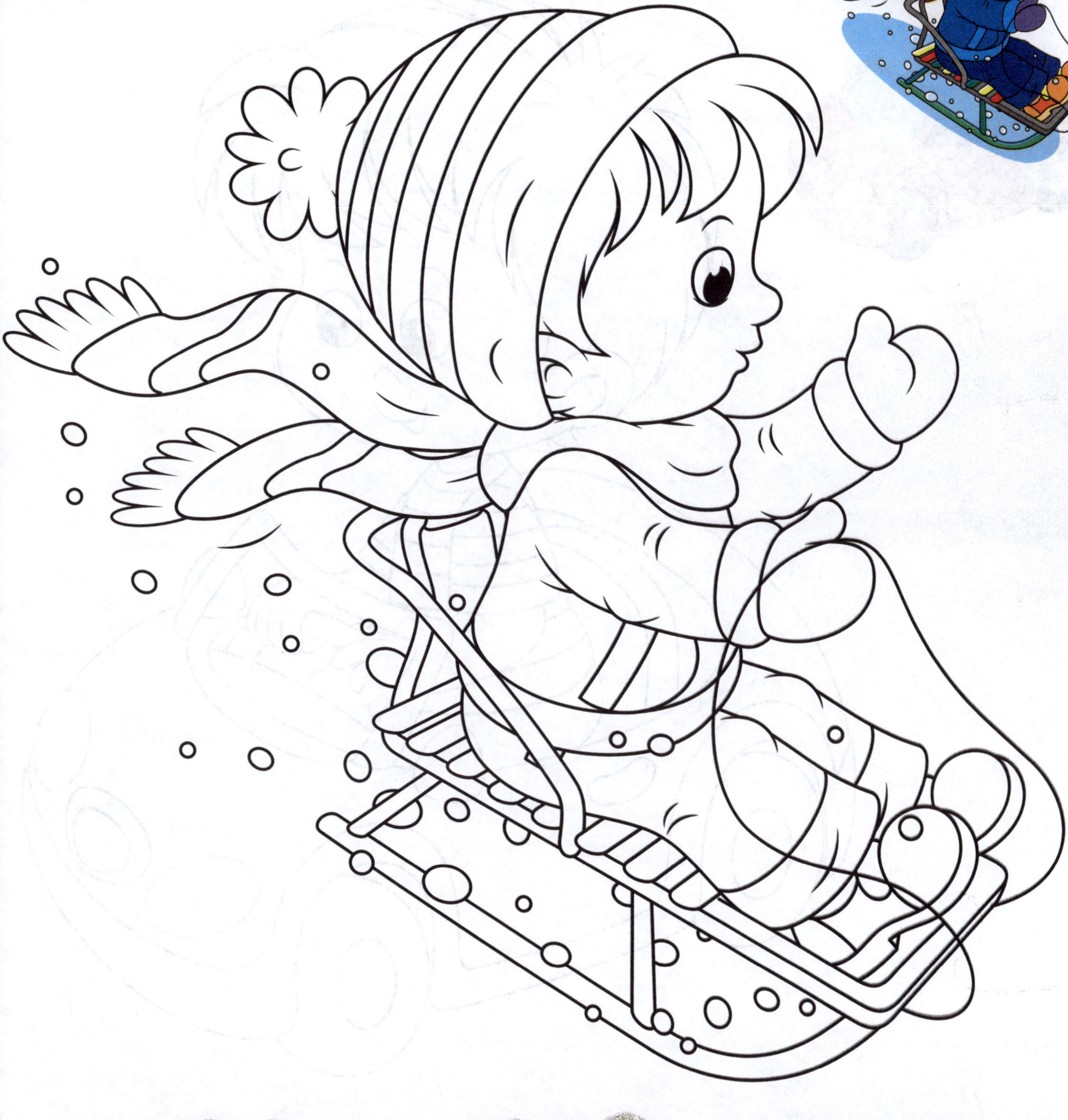

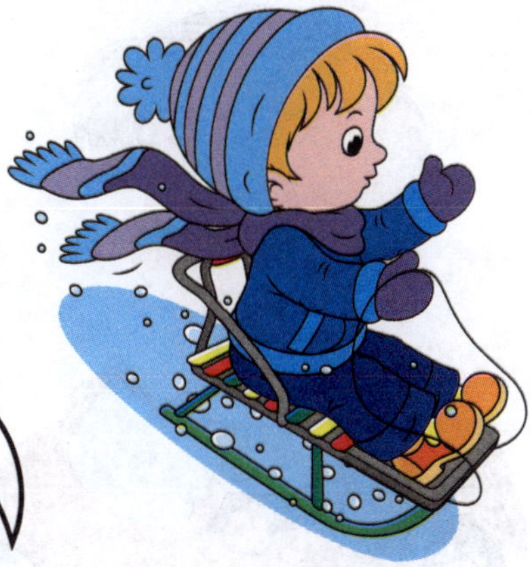

sleighing

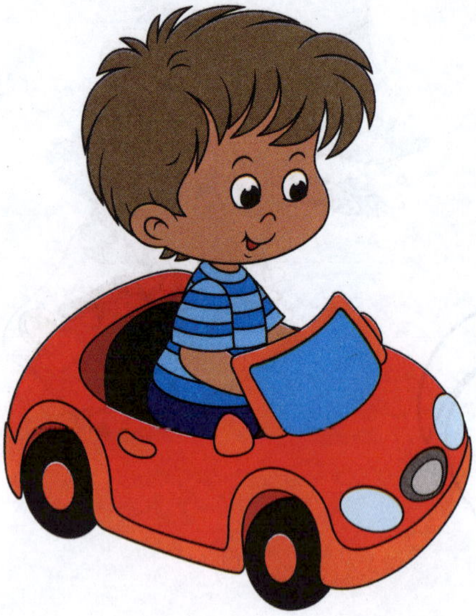

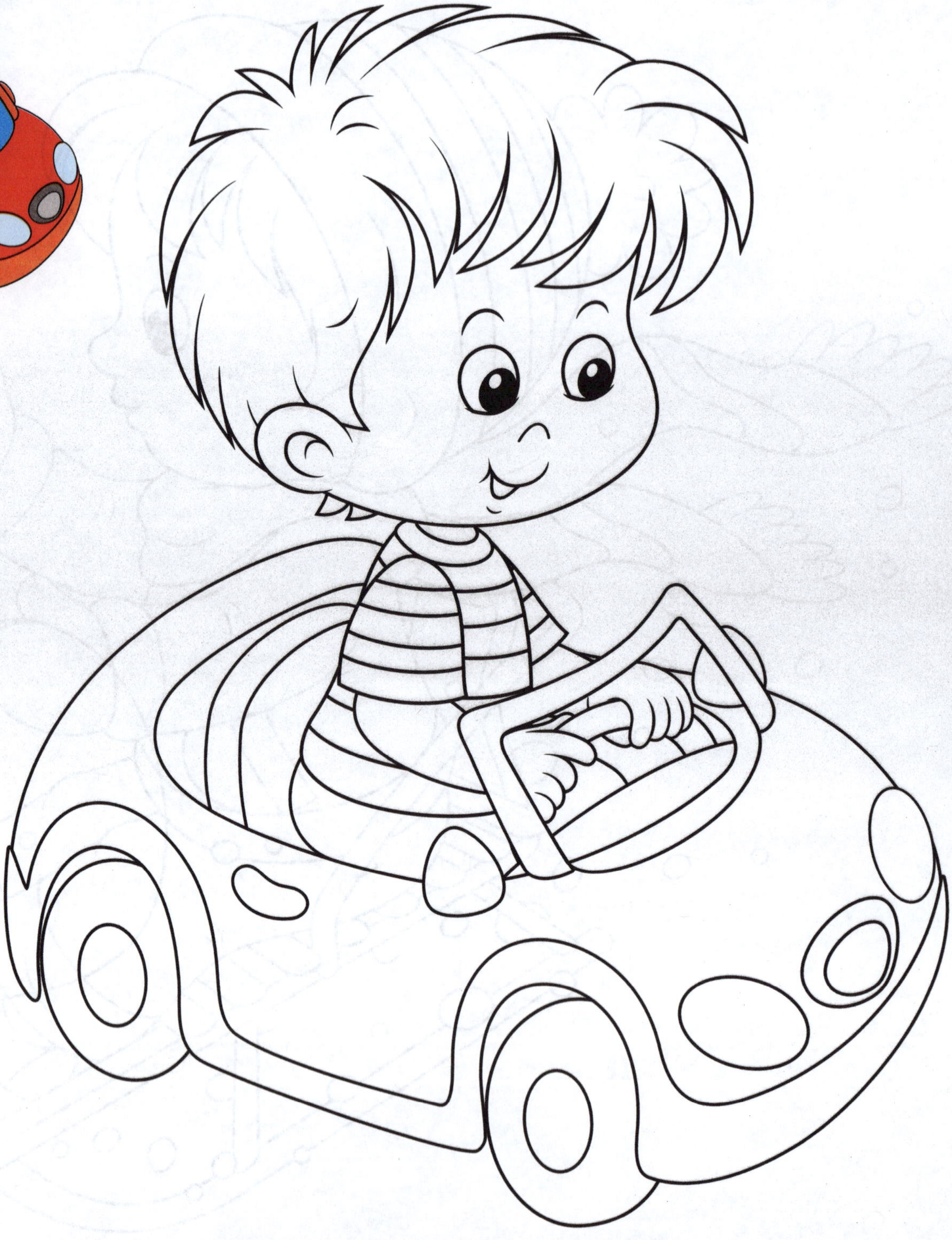

racing